Wanderer

Wanderer

Written by Kyung-Mo Kim
Illustrated by Ye-Rin Jo

가림출판사

Acknowledgement

A son. A student. A traveler. An observer. I am many things. In this poetry book, I try to share my experiences of traveling and living in so many wonderful places thanks to my father, a respectful diplomat.

The writing process was fun but sometimes hard. I know without the support and encouragement from my loved ones, finishing this book would have been impossible.

I want to thank my Mom and my sister, for introducing new ideas when I faced writer's block. I also want to thank my cousin, Ye-Rin Jo, for her beautiful illustrations.
Last but not least, I sincerely thank Ms.Chang, my writing teacher, for assisting me throughout the whole process.

August 15, 2018
Kyung-Mo Kim

길지 않은 인생이지만 난 운이 좋았다.

특별한 부모님의 아들로, 학생으로, 여행자로 또 관찰자로서 나는 여러 역할을 하며 살아왔다.

또한 여러 나라에서 살며 여행을 통해 얻은 많은 경험과 추억을 가질 수 있었다.

그리고 이 모든 것이 시가 되었다.

독특한 나만의 시간을 가질 수 있게 해주신 대한민국의 훌륭한 외교관이신 나의 아버지께 감사드린다.

시를 쓰는 과정은 재미있었지만 때로는 어려움이 있었고, 그런 나에게 용기를 주고 응원해주신 많은 분들께 감사드린다.

시적 영감을 얻기 위해 고민할 때 새로운 생각으로 이끌어주신 어머니, 그리고 내 동생 민서에게 감사의 마음을 전하고, 멋진 표지 그림을 그려준 예린이 누나에게 특별한 감사를 전한다.

그리고 마지막으로 이 책을 낼 수 있도록 끝까지 손을 잡아주신 나의 선생님, 장문정 선생님께 진심으로 감사드린다.

2018년 여름

김경모

Table of Contents

Learning

배움

Living

일상

Wandering

방랑

Wind Shoes

The journey didn't begin

Until the shoes of Hermes came to me

Like Rimbaud traveling with his wind shoes

I started my trip in my little shoes

Crossing the clouds, I went to Europe

Reaching for the sky, I arrived in Africa

The world is an enormous paradise

So, there are still a lot to enjoy

바람구두

헤르메스의 날개 달린 신발이 내게로 오기 전까지
여행은 시작되지 않았다
바람구두를 신고 여행하는 랭보처럼
나는 작은 신발을 신고 여행을 시작한다
구름을 가로질러 유럽에 닿고
하늘을 건너 아프리카에 도착했다
세상은 거대한 낙원
그래, 즐길 것들이 여전히 남아있다

2002 World Cup

When we start to gather

The town turns red

As we cheer like the thunder

We get closer to our dream

2002 When I was born

2002 월드컵

우리가 함께였을 때
세상은 붉게 물들었고
우리가 천둥처럼 소리지를 때
꿈은 이루어졌다
내가 태어났던 그 해 2002년

Swiss Alps

I see a mountain

Hiding in the clouds

White as cream

High as sky

What will it be like

If I climb to the top?

As I sit on the train that goes up the Alps

I wonder

알프스 산악열차

산을 바라본다
구름 속에 숨은
크림처럼 하얀 눈이 덮인
하늘만큼 높은
그 꼭대기에 오르면
어떻게 보일까?
나는 알프스에 오르는 산악열차에 앉아
하염없이 감탄한다

Raspberry Bush

On the giant backyard

A raspberry bush was in the center

I sometimes ate its berries

I sometimes played with them

Now I'm away from Switzerland

I can only miss that bush

An unforgettable place in my childhood

라즈베리 덤불

알프스 품은 넓다란 뒷마당
한 귀퉁이 라즈베리 덤불
가끔 붉은 열매를 따먹기도 하고
가끔 놀이터가 되어준 곳
그곳을 떠나온 뒤
내가 할 수 있는 것은 그리워하는 것뿐
내 유년의 아련한 기억 속 그곳

Victoria Fall

A gigantic waterfall connecting two countries in Africa

The thundering roar as big as the fall

Stunned by the huge rainbow hanging over the waterfall

I once again realize how small humans are

---

*Victoria Fall is a waterfall in southern Africa on the Zambezi River at the border between Zambia and Zimbabwe.

빅토리아 폭포

아프리카 검은 땅 두 나라에 걸쳐진 거대한 폭포
포효하는 사자처럼 울부짖는다
폭포 위에 걸쳐진 신비한 무지개 아래에 선 나는
할 말을 잃는다
아, 나는 얼마나 작은 존재인가?

Great Zimbabwe

When animals are peacefully roaming around

A horn echoes the plain

They scurry back to the cave

Where they hide when the warriors come

One of the warriors start to roar like a lion

Then others follow him

Clang Clang Clang

Panic surrounds the animals

But when the fight ends

And the moon brightens the sky

Everything becomes peaceful

Like there hasn't been anything

They carefully come out one by one from the cave

And peace continues

---

*Zimbabwe is a landlocked country located in southern Africa.

그레이트 짐바브웨

동물들이 한가로이 어슬렁거릴때
뿔나팔 소리 평온에 메아리 친다
포식자가 다가올 시간
그들은 잰 걸음으로 동굴로 돌아가 숨는다
사자가 울부짖기 시작하면
모두 그를 따라 포효한다
아~ 우~
초원의 동물들은 혼비백산
하지만 싸움이 끝나고
하늘에 달이 세상을 비추면
모든 것이 다시 평화롭다
마치 아무일 없었다는 듯
그들은 하나 둘 조심스레 굴을 나서고
평화가 그곳에 머문다

USA

Houses are big

Land is wide

People are huge

The coke is gigantic

Foods come out enormous

Everything here is big

미국

큰 집
드넓은 땅덩이
덩치 큰 사람들
큰 컵에 담긴 콜라
한 접시에 그득한 음식
모든 것이 커다란 이곳

Two Koreas

Two different countries

Two different life styles

Two different governments

But

We have the same ancestors

We talk the same language

We are one family

The countries aren't yet united

But I wish I could visit unified Korea

두 개의 한국

전혀 다른 두 나라가 있다
전혀 다른 두 삶의 방식이 있다
전혀 다른 두 정부가 있다
그러나,
우린 같은 조상을 가지고
우린 같은 언어를 쓰고
우린 한겨레다
두 나라는 아직 하나되지 못했지만
나는 하나 된 코리아에 꼭 가고 싶다

Carsick

When will I arrive?

When can I get out of this car?

Listening to music

I'm too bored

With nothing to do

Out on the field

I see cows dancing in freedom

I wish I could join them

멀미

언제까지 가야 되지?
언제 내릴 수 있을까?
음악을 들어도
지루하기만 하고
아무것도 할 게 없어
밖을 내다보면
너른 들판에 소들이 자유롭게 춤춘다
차라리 쟤들과 함께 하고 싶네

Next Destination

Will I go to the Sahara Desert?

Or will I see the Amazon jungle?

Will I face the freezing winter?

Or will I encounter the sweltering heat?

I always get curious

When I have to leave

아빠의 다음 발령지

사하라 사막으로 가나?
아님, 아마존 밀림을 보나?
얼어붙은 추위를 만나려나?
아님, 찌는 더위를 마주할까?
언제나 궁금해
떠나야 할 때가 되면

Observing

관찰

Starry Night

When the crickets chirp

And fireflies glow

Serene night covers the world

I sit on the dancing grasses

Hoping to reach one star

별이 빛나는 밤

귀뚜라미 울 때
반딧불이 불을 밝히고
고요한 밤은 세상을 덮는다
나는 춤추는 풀밭 위에 앉았다
어느 별에 다다르기를 바라며

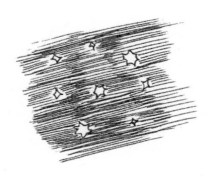

My Moon

You light up the night

When I'm lost

Some say you're cold

But I feel your warmth

Years later

I promise you

That I will meet you in the space

나의 달

당신은 밤을 비추지
내가 길을 잃을까 봐
어떤 이는 당신이 차갑다 하지만
난 당신의 따스함을 느껴
머지않아
난 당신을 만나러 갈 거야
약속해

The Dawn of May

When no one is awake

I go out alone

Passing through the forest

I breath in the morning air

The scent of the wet soil

The aroma of the green foxtail

The lazy breath tells me it's the start of May

Humming with the birds

I wait for the sun

오월의 새벽

아직 아무도 일어나지 않은 시간
나는 홀로 밖을 나선다
숲을 가로질러
새벽 공기를 들이킨다
젖은 흙내
초록 강아지풀 냄새 코끝을 간지르고
게으른 호흡이 오월의 첫날임을 알린다
새들은 지저귀고
나는 해를 기다린다

Dandelion Seed

When the time comes

They are ready to travel

Saying good bye

They start their journey

They will never meet again

But watching them leave doesn't feel sad at all

민들레 홀씨

시간이 됐어
여행을 떠날 시간이야
준비가 됐어
작별인사를 하고
여행을 시작해
다시는 만날 수 없겠지
하지만 서로 멀어지는 걸 보며
슬픔은 전혀 없는 듯

What a Lovely Day

What a lovely day

The sky is dull and gray

The rain falls like a sea of tears

Wind blows the house with its anger

The power is out

And the devices are all shut

Only thing I can do

Is to look out the window

What a lovely day!

어느 멋진 날에

낮게 드리운 회색빛 하늘
비는 바다가 흘리는 눈물처럼 쏟아지고
분노로 가득찬 바람이 창문을 두드린다
순간 암전!
모든 것이 꺼져버린 그때
내가 할 수 있는 유일한 일
뛰는 가슴으로 창 밖을 응시하는 일
이 얼마나 멋진 날인지!

Sun

When the sun comes out to shine

Everything awakes

Birds start to twitter

Plants start to grow

Flowers start to bloom

As if it controls the time

The sun invites the morning

태양

태양이 빛을 뿌리기 시작하면
모든 것이 잠에서 깬다
새들은 지저귀고
풀들은 자라나고
꽃들이 봉오리를 피운다
마치 시간을 조정하는 것처럼
태양이 아침을 부른다

Shongololo

The scariest creature in Africa

Black as a devil

Long as a 30cm ruler

Thick as an Elmer's glue

With thousands of legs

They creep out after a rainy day

And die by sunlight

Shongololo

The real-world zombies

---

*Shongololo is an African centipede.

청고롤로

아프리카의 무서운 생명체
악마처럼 검고
자처럼 길고
액체풀처럼 찐득한
천 개의 다리로
젖은 땅 위에 꿈틀거린다
햇빛아래 시체가 된
청고롤로
이 세상에 나타난 진정한 좀비

Cat

You don't think

You don't work

You don't leave

You just eat

You just play

And sleep

What a great life you have!

고양이

생각이 없는 듯
딱히 하는 일도 없이
남의 집에서 떠나지 않는다
그저 먹고
그저 놀고
또 자고
네가 가진 **뻔뻔한** 멋진 삶이 마냥 부러울 뿐

Sun at 7am

Seems like you want to play with me

But you are an unwelcomed guest

Please don't come to me

아침 7시 태양

신나서 음악까지 울리며
나랑 놀려고 오는 너
하지만 넌 환영받지 못하는 손님
제발 내게 오지 말아줘

Nocturnal

When others play
And the world is bright
We sleep

When others go to bed
And the sky gets dark
We start moving

Some say we are extraordinary
Some say we are weird
But if you want to join us in the dark
You're always welcome

밤도깨비

세상이 밝고
모두가 움직일 때
우리는 잠이 들어

하늘이 어두워지고
모두가 잠자리에 들 때
우린 움직이기 시작하지

누군가 우리를 특이하다고
누군가 우릴 괴상하다고
하지만 당신이 어둠 속으로 함께 하겠다면
우린 언제나 환영이야

Bad Beach

The wet sand never leaves my feet clean

Too many people

Too loud music

The waves chill my body cold

Seashells cut my feet

Why do people love the beach?

Why?

한심한 바닷가

젖은 모래는 내 발에 들러붙고
너무 많은 사람들과
너무 시끄러운 음악
파도는 내 몸을 차갑게 얼리고
조개에 발까지 베었는데
사람들은 왜 바닷가를 좋아하는 거지?
도대체 왜!

Autumn

Sometimes hot like summer

Sometimes cold like winter

I can see leaves turning red

But I can't tell you apart

Autumn

Who are you?

가을

여름인 듯 덥기도
겨울인 듯 춥기도
붉게 물들기 시작하는 잎으로만 알 수 있는
온전히 느껴지지 않는 어중간함
가을
넌 누구냐?

Christmas

Kids go play in the snow
Making snow angels with joy

Couples meet together
And have the happiest day in the year

Jingle bells ring through the town
Singing Christmas carols outside

My friends call me to play
But I don't go anywhere
Because I'm in love with my fireplace

크리스마스

아이들은 눈밭을 뒹굴며
눈 위에 날개짓으로 천사가 된다

연인들은 서로 만나
가장 행복한 하루를 보낸다

징글벨이 거리마다 흘러나오고
사람들은 캐롤을 흥얼거린다

친구들은 나를 불러대지만
나에게 필요한 건 따뜻한 벽난로 옆에서
오로지 나만을 위해 즐기는 느긋한 시간

Learning

배움

Chain Effect

Smith brothers didn't show up last week

Jimmy was absent yesterday

Sara isn't here today

Feeling cold and dizzy

I might be the next

After all

It's the flu season

연쇄작용

스미스 형제가 지난주에 안 보였어
지미가 어제 결석했고
사라도 오늘 안 보이는데
몸이 으실으실 어지럽네
그럼 내가 다음 차례?
지금은 감기 시즌

Snow Day

Weatherman says it's going to snow

But I still feel anxious

The sky is gray

The clouds are dark

But I don't see snow

Reloading the Gmail every minute

I nervously wait for the message

"No school tomorrow"

---

*Snow day is the United States and Canada is a day that school classes are cancelled or delayed by snow.

스노우 데이

일기예보에서 눈이 온대
아직은 완전히 믿을 순 없지
하늘은 분명 잿빛이고
구름이 낮게 드리우고
그런데 아직은 아니야
수시로 누르고 있는 이메일 새로 고침
지루하도록 기다리는 메시지
"내일 학교가 쉽니다"

Crescent

A god never rolls a dice

And never gives a chance twice

Every time I take a test

He always gives me a quest

To figure out what I will get

This time the omen was a crescent in the sky

That I spot with dread

Slapping my face with a clout

Finally figured out

That I got a C

초승달

신은 주사위를 굴리지 않아
두 번 기회를 주지도 않지
매 순간 난 시험에 들었고
신은 언제나 내게 질문을 해댔지
내가 받을 것이 무엇인지 알게 되기까지

이 시간 하늘에 뜬 초승달은 하나의 징조
불안은 극에 달하고
내 뺨을 찰싹 때리며
마침내 발견한
C학점

English and Math

You need to learn a new language

                              No need to learn a new language

There is no fixed answers to questions

                              There is always the right answer

Questions are ambiguous

                              Questions are straightforward

With essays every quarter

                              With formulas to memorize

English is hard

                              Math is easy!

영어 vs 수학

새로운 언어를 배워야 해

새로운 언어는 필요 없어

질문에 대한 정답은 없지

질문에 대한 정답은 꼭 있어

애매모호한 질문

딱 떨어지는 질문

매 학기 내야 하는 에세이

공식암기 적용 끝

영어 패!

수학 승!

Pledge of Allegiance

I pledge of allegiance to the flag of United States of America...

This is all I know

The words are too many

And I'm too lazy

Although I will do this for rest of my school year

I don't think I can memorize all of it

국기에 대한 맹세

나는 미합중국 깃발 앞에 충성을 맹세한다...
이것이 내가 아는 전부
원래는 훨씬 길지만
내가 좀 게으른 건가
미국 학교 다니는 남은 시간 동안
다 외울 수 있을지 모르겠네

English Honors 10

My new nightmare

More timed essays

More debates

More readings

More tests

As I suffered the 9th English Honors

I can only fear what's coming next

---

*English Honors courses generally refer to exclusive, higher-level classes
that proceed at a faster pace and cover more material than regular classes.

영어 아너스 10

내 새로운 악몽
더 많은 에세이
더 많은 디베이트
더 많은 리딩
더 많은 시험
9학년 간신히 마쳤는데 10학년 시작
끝나도 끝난 것이 아닌 두려운 영어시간

International School

Some are white
Some are black

Some are loud
Some are quiet

Some believe in Buddha
Some believe in Jesus

Some are born here
Some are from abroad

But we all play together
We study together
We smile together
We dream together

We are all different
But we are same

인터내셔널 스쿨

어떤 애는 희고
어떤 애는 검다

어떤 애는 시끄럽고
어떤 애는 조용하다

어떤 애는 부처를
어떤 애는 예수를 믿는다

어떤 애는 여기서 태어났고
어떤 애는 외국에서 왔다

그래도 함께 놀고
함께 공부하고
함께 웃으며
함께 꿈꾼다

우린 모두 다르지만
우린 모두 똑같다

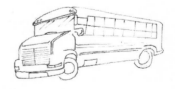

Free Cafeteria Lunch

Students have to study

Have homework

Have to sleep early

Have to compete each other

Adults get to earn money by working

Have holidays

Have business trips

Have fun parties

But being a student is better

Since we eat free cafeteria lunch!

공짜 점심

학생들은 공부해야만 하고
숙제해야만 하고
일찍 자야만 하고
서로 경쟁해야만 하는데

어른들은 일하면서 돈도 벌고
휴일도 즐기고
출장 겸 여행도 가고
재미있는 파티도 즐기지

그래도 학생이어서 좋은 점 하나
공짜 점심을 먹는 일!

Last Day of Summer Break

Summer break has gone too fast

Taking my memories of past

It feels like yesterday

But it ends tomorrow

Dreading the Monday

It only gives me sorrow

여름방학 마지막 날

여름 방학이 휙 가버렸다
돌이켜 생각해 봐도
시작이 어제처럼 느껴지는데
내일이 끝이라니
두려운 월요일
슬프고도 슬프다

Winter Break

2 weeks

Comes like wind

Melts like snow

겨울방학

달랑 2주
바람처럼 왔다
눈처럼 녹는 시간

Graduation

Good bye my friends
It's time for us to part

Good bye my teachers
What you taught will never be forgotten

Good bye school
The bell rings sadly as if it's replying to me

I walk through the front door for the last time
With all the memories of school life in my heart

졸업

굿바이 친구들
이젠 우리가 헤어질 시간이야

굿바이 선생님
가르쳐 주신 많은 것들 잊지 않겠습니다

굿바이 나의 학교
종소리도 안녕하며 슬피 울리네

학교에서의 모든 추억을 마음 한편에 묻고
마지막으로 교문을 나선다

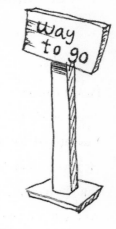

Living

일상

Sweet Potato

Peaceful night

Sweet aroma lures my nose

I see an old man selling baked sweet potatoes

He says it's a dollar

But I have only 2 quarters

As I sadly turn around

He smiles and gives me one sweet potato

I still remember his kind smile

군고구마

평화로운 밤
어디선가 달콤한 냄새
내 눈을 사로잡은 군고구마 할아버지
따끈한 군고구마가 1달러
내 손에는 달랑 동전 두 개뿐
아쉽게 돌아서는 순간,
웃으며 내 손에 올려주신 군고구마
그 온기보다 더 따스한 할아버지의 달콤한 미소

Promise

Making a promise is like forming a new friendship

Once you share the promise

You and he become one

But once you break that promise

Friendship is break

Since you have cut the tie

약속

약속이란 새로운 우정을 만드는 과정
당신과 내가 약속을 지키면
우리는 서로에게 친구가 된다

당신과 내가 약속을 어기면
우정은 금이 가고
우리는 서로에게 이방인이 된다

Traffic Jam

Cars are like us

As they get crowded

Jamming the road

Our hearts feel frustrated

Blaming one another

교통지옥

차와 사람들로 가득찬 거리
차들은 뒤엉킨다
심장박동 올라가고
점점 더 커지는 경적소리
여기가 바로 지옥

Shower

Every sweaty night
The bathroom becomes a theater

Shower head sprays water enthusiastically
And the bubbles from the soap dance in the air

Every sweaty night
I become the best singer in the world!

샤워

달콤하게 젖는 밤
샤워부스는 나만의 전용극장

물줄기는 열정적으로 쏟아지고
비눗방울은 춤추기 시작한다

달콤하게 젖는 밤
세상에서 가장 멋진 가수가 된다

Black Friday

Eyes tremble

Heartbeat fastens

Cold sweat soaks me

Hiccups never end

With a one last gulp

The decision has been made

블랙 프라이데이

눈은 휘둥그레
심장박동은 쿵쾅
식은땀이 촉촉
거기다 딸꾹질까지
크게 침 한 번 삼키고
마침내 결제 성공!

Dentist

I thought we were going to the amusement park
I should have noticed her wicked grin
Driving in the heavy rain
I opened the giant gloomy door

Then a familiar smell that I hate stung my nose
My body started to shiver
Kids were crying desperately
And there comes the tall, hairy man
In a white shiny goun
Holding a deadly weapon
Making the same grin like Mom made
And called my name

I shouldn't have believed her
I should have stayed at home

My worst nightmare just began!

치과

우리는 놀이동산에 가는 것이라고 했다
하지만 난 엄마의 비밀스런 미소를 보고 말았다
빗속을 뚫고 도착한 그곳
무겁고 침울해 보이는 문을 열었다

코를 자극하는 끔찍한 냄새에
몸이 떨려오기 시작한다
아이들의 절망적인 절규가 들린다
하얗게 날세운 가운을 입고
끔찍한 연장을 손에 든
크고 험악한 남자가 걸어온다
그가 나의 이름을 부른다

난 엄마를 믿지 말았어야 했다
난 집에 머물렀어야만 했다

그리고는 시작된 끔찍한 악몽!

416(Sewol Ferry)

It is easy to forget things

Even all those tragic events

The world still moves on forgetting things

When one's smile never comes back

---

*The sinking of MV Sewol, also referred to as the Sewol Ferry Disaster, occurred on the morning of 16 April 2014.

416(세월호)

아무리 끔찍한 비극이었을지라도
잊혀져 가는 건 쉬운 일
세상은 잊으며 계속 움직이고 있다
하지만 결코 돌아올 수 없는 누군가의 미소를
잊을 수 있을까?

Undeletable Memories

Too many sad memories

In elementary school

They don't leave me alone

I fear they may last

Punching pillows doesn't help

When I'm haunted by my child hood memories

흑역사

무수히 많은 슬픈 기억 중에
절대 잊혀지지 않는
계속 뇌리에 스며드는
나의 초등학교 시절
잊으려 베개에 머리를 파묻어도
점점 더 또렷해지는 잊고 싶은 나의 흑역사

Drowsiness

My eyes don't obey me

My mind ditches me every time

My body feels like it's not mine

My blanket and pillow whisper me to come back

And the only thing I think about

Is to go back in the bed

졸음

내 눈이 스르르 감겨온다
내 정신이 매 순간 멀어져 간다
내 몸이 내 것이 아닌 것처럼 느껴진다
이불과 베개는 나에게 어서 오라 속삭이고
지금 이순간 내가 생각할 수 있는 유일한 것
침대로 달려가기

First Love

When I opened my eyes

The calm hushing wind kissed my cheek

Then I noticed that I was in a flower garden

As I walked through the isle

Another wind, which smelled like roses surrounded me

I turned to the way where the wind blew

Then, I saw a girl

Her skin as pale as a baby

Her clothes were the Aphrodite's dress

But after I blinked once, the girl was gone

I rubbed my eyes again and again

Until I spotted a familiar ceiling

Then I realized that my little sister was playing with the fan

첫사랑

눈을 떴을 때
조용히 속삭이는 바람이 볼을 간지르고
난 꽃밭 한가운데 누워 있다

꽃길을 따라 걸을 때
장미향 머금은 바람이 주변을 맴돈다.

향기를 따라 돌아섰을 때
아기처럼 순수하고
아프로디테의 드레스를 휘감은
한 소녀가 내 앞에 서 있다

눈을 깜박인 순간 그녀가 사라진다
계속해서 눈을 비벼보지만
보이는 건 익숙한 내 방 천장

그 순간 옆에서 장난치듯 부채질하고 있는
동생이 나를 깨운다

Nightmare

In my dream
I always scream
Frightened by ghost
Zombies the most
When I wake up
And see the window
A shadow appears

Giving me fear
I try to shout
I try to move
But it doesn't work
I stay still

When I open my eyes
Nothing is there
And I only see sunshine

악몽

꿈에서
난 항상 소리친다
유령이 놀라게 하고
좀비가 쫓는다
일어나서 창문을 보면
어두운 그림자가 공포에 떨게 한다

나는 소리치고 싶다
나는 움직이고 싶다
나는 아무것도 할 수가 없다
나는 꼼짝없이 누워 있다

다행히 다시 눈을 떠보면
아무도 없다
이건 단지 악몽!

Life

Life is like cooking

The flavor changes every time we add a spice

Sometimes bitter

Sometimes sweet

There are many ups and downs in life

But adding a spice

The flavor will turn

And it will get more delicious

맛있는 인생

인생은 요리다
어떤 향신료를 더하는지에 따라
맛이 변한다
어떨 땐 쓰고
어떨 땐 달콤하다

인생에도 다양한 맛이 있다
노력 한 스푼 더하면 그 맛이 변하고
더 맛있는 삶이 된다

Wanderer

2018년 8월 15일 제1판 1쇄 발행

글 / 김경모
그림 / 조예린
펴낸이 / 강선희
펴낸곳 / 가림출판사

등록 / 1992. 10. 6. 제 4-191호
주소 / 서울시 광진구 영화사로 83-1(구의동) 영진빌딩 5층
대표전화 / 02)458-6451 팩스 / 02)458-6450
홈페이지 / www.galim.co.kr
이메일 / galim@galim.co.kr

값 6,000원

ⓒ 김경모, 조예린, 2018

ISBN 978-89-7895-411-2 03800